To my very
friend,
Jass
my spiritual sister.
If I can do it so
can you!

Love
for Ja.

Souls Colliding
A Story Of Two Souls Lost And Found

Beverley Dawson

authorHOUSE®

AuthorHouse™ UK Ltd.
500 Avebury Boulevard
Central Milton Keynes, MK9 2BE
www.authorhouse.co.uk
Phone: 08001974150

© 2009 Beverley Dawson. All rights reserved.

No part of this book may be reproduced, stored in a retrieval system, or transmitted by any means without the written permission of the author.

First published by AuthorHouse 5/5/2009

ISBN: 978-1-4389-7835-2 (sc)

This book is printed on acid-free paper.

I dedicate this book to one very special person because without his help, both on the earth plain and in spirit, I would not have achieved all I have today.

You're the place my life began

And you'll be where it ends……

Prologue

John was dead. Today was his funeral. Flora had been dreading it.

How was she going to cope? How was she going to contain her tears and not draw attention to herself?

They had said goodbye eight weeks ago and now here she was sitting in her car, far enough away not to be noticed but close enough outside the church, to wait for her two friends and more importantly the arrival of the coffin carrying her soul mate.

"You have spent too much on the flowers"

Flowers! Said Flora. I haven't bought any flowers. "Well", said the medium, "he said you have spent too much"..

Flora had planned to go to the florist following her reading. What a strange thing to say. How did she know that?

"There will be a single pink rose in amongst them. He wants you to retrieve it and keep it for him"

"Ok" said Flora, rather intrigued by it all.

Flora had been told about this women and how good she was at communicating with people who had passed over.

John died 10 days ago so she wasn't expecting too much. But she knew she had to try anything she could just to have another chance to say goodbye, hear from him one last time.

"He will be there watching and he says he will give you a sign that he is", the medium went on to say. "Their all hypocrites, he's saying. especially her. No emotion at all. You'll see". He's quite bitter about it.

Flora was suddenly bought back to the here and now with a loud tapping on her window. Her two friends had arrived.

"Oh my god"! She yelled, "You made me jump"

"You ok"? They asked.

Yes. She replied getting out of the car. Shall we go in?

Her flowers had already been sent to the undertaker by the floral company. She had no idea what her flowers were like and she did spend too much just as he had said! But as the newspaper announcement had said Small Garden Flowers only,

Flora stopped off on her way to the church to purchase a small bunch of sweet Williams also.

As they entered the church Flora stopped almost tripping her friends up who were behind her.. There he was there was her soul mate lying in the coffin at the front of the church. She hadn't expected that. She had assumed he would be carried in after everyone was seated. But then this was a Roman Catholic funeral and she had never been to one before. Flora walked towards the coffin and placed her Sweet Williams on the top. Both Mary and Jane looked at each other. You can't do that!" Said Mary

"Why?" Said Flora. "Family flowers only" they replied. "Well I can't take them off now people are watching" she replied "come on lets sit down.

Flora didn't know yet, but her flowers were to be the sign John had been talking about.

"Room 42 Mr John Atherton aged 57 for Mr Marshland. Right total knee replacement this afternoon. He returned to the ward at

19.30pm. Past medical history Spinal fusion 3 years ago."

It was the start of Floras night shift and she was in the office having hand over from the day shift.

"He has an infusion of normal saline running over 8 hours into the cannula of his left wrist. He has a drain in his right knee with approx 200mls blood loss so far. If total drainage exceeds 700mls then he has 2 units of blood prescribed. Intravenous antibiotics due at 01.00hrs and 08.00hrs. For pain relief a morphine pump (PCA) is in situ. Lock out period 5mins. He is managing to control pain himself he appears comfortable at the moment."

Room 43 Mrs ......report went on.

Flora didn't hear any more of the handover. She knew the previous name had meant something but couldn't think why.

"And finally room 45. FLORA shouted staff nurse Cox. Have you heard anything of the handover given for the past 3 patients?" Flora, startled by the sudden loud voice, came back into the here and now. "Sorry. I was listening honest" she said.

I hope so, remarked the Staff nurse as she got up to leave the office, they are your patients' tonight. Have a good night and I will see you in the morning said Suzie Cox as she left the ward.

"What was that all about then Flora where did you drift of to in handover?" Laura asked.

"I don't know. It was strange really the name John Atherton got me thinking but I can't for the life of me think why it should." She replied.

"Well said Laura you may will find out very soon as he's your patient tonight". "Maybe she said" as she made her way to his room." Hello she said I'm Flora your nurse for the night.

Having only recently returned to the ward from theatre he was still very sleepy. She wasn't sure he had heard a word she'd said. But she went on to check his drain and marked the loss on the bottle. This would give an indication of how much he was loosing and whether he would need the blood transfusion later on. She checked his drug and observation charts and as she did so he woke up. "Hello" he said.

"Hello she replied. How are you feeling?

"Not too bad as it goes I am not in any pain at the moment" he said.

"That's good" she said as she proceeded to monitor his blood pressure pulse and respiration rate and record them on his chart for 9.o'clock.

She informed him that she had other patients to settle but she would return to check on him and monitor his observations again in an hour and he was to ring his bell if he needed her before.

John thanked her and drifted back of to sleep.

The lights went down at 23.00hrs. All was calm and feeling as though it could be a relatively quiet night ahead.

"Coffee time" shouted Lucy is everyone ready for one? "Yes"! The reply came in unison.

Just at that moment John rang his bell. Flora got up of her chair to answer it.

"How can I help you"? She asked as she turned of his call bell.

"I know you were about to have coffee he replied but I'm itching terribly.

Flora pulled back the bed covers to investigate further. He was covered in a rash radiating down both arms and across his chest.

"It appears you are having a reaction to the morphine she told him. It can be one of the side effects. I am expecting the Doctor down shortly so I will have a word and see if I can get you an alternative pain relief prescribed" and you can stop using the morphine.

"Thank you Flora, he said, but I'm not in any pain at the moment so don't worry". "No but you may experience some later if we stop your morphine. You will need something else to control the pain then" she replied"?

Flora left his room and went over to the nurses' station. The girls were enjoying their coffee.

"Has the doctor been down yet" she asked.

"Been and gone" they replied.

"Oh no, I need him now. Better phone him then. Who is it tonight"?

"Justin!!! They said, rather you than me"!

Doctor Filer was the most arrogant unapproachable man at the best of times, so at 23.45pm he was not going to be happy to be called!

"Oh well here goes" she said.

Flora dialled his room number and waited for his reply.

"Hi Justin Flora here. I am sorry to call you. I know you have already been down but I have a patient who is reacting to the morphine in his P.C.A. He is itching and has a rash on his arms, and chest. He really needs his pain relief reviewed if I am to turn the pump off and may be some antihistamines prescribing to stop the itching".

"Why are you turning off the pump? He said.

"Well, said Flora. The hospital policy says. If a patient has an allergic reaction to the morphine we are to turn off the pump and seek alternative analgesia".

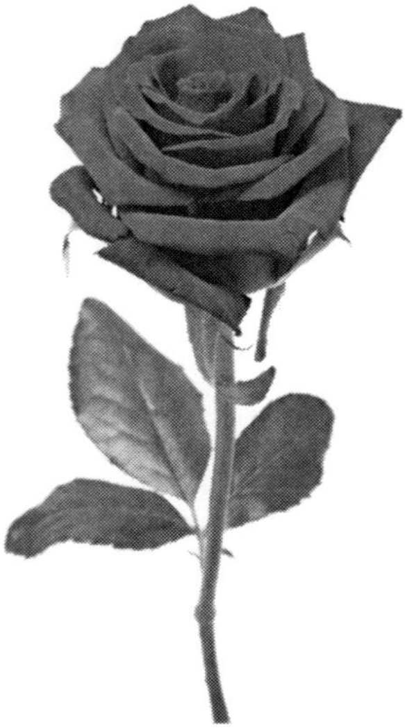

"Well Flora I am telling you not to turn off the pump. Just give him an antihistamine and I'll write it up in the morning".

"That's just typical of that man, she said angrily putting down the phone. Can you believe it? He said no to turning of the pump, no to coming down and no to prescribing alternative analgesia."

It was nothing more than she had expected but it didn't help her or her patient.

She went and got the antihistamine for John and took it to him.

This would relieve the itching she told him. But unfortunately would do nothing for the pain.

As John's room was close to the nurses' station he had heard most of the conversation she'd had with the doctor. "Thank you Flora" "Thank you for trying. I heard most of that you did your best now go and get your coffee I'll ring the bell if I need anything"! He said.

Flora felt awful. But all she could do now was make sure John had a comfortable post-operative night. She made sure he was as comfortable as he could be she until the end of her shift.

When Flora returned to work three nights later. John was up and about. The events of that post- op night were long behind him. He was pleased to see her.

John wasn't her patient that night. But once she had settled her patients, Flora went to spend some time with him. John informed her that he didn't sleep well in hospital so they talked long into the night about anything and everything and she made him endless cups of tea. She found him fascinating. He had certainly lead a full and active life.

She discovered he was a fashion photographer and had photographed many famous top models in his time at many interesting locations. He told her how hard the fashion industry was for the model working long hours for 100% perfection and very little pay. Magazines his work had been featured in. Flora took it all in. John told her about his first ever experience of this hospital. He had fallen of a platform during a photo shoot and injured his back he had needed complicated back surgery to correct the damage. It was at that moment she remembered why this man's name had got her wandering in report last week. It was about 3years ago he went on to say. "That's it" she said out loud. Sorry said John, "I missed that what did you say?"

Flora hadn't nursed him but had been unfortunate in having to do the early morning ward round of all his particular surgeons' spinal patients. It was something each of the night nurses dreaded as it usually meant you were the one leaving work late that morning.

On that particular morning the ward round seemed to be taking longer than usual. Mr Webster had wanted to chat with every patient for some reason this was not always the case. By the time they had reached room 27, Mr Atherton, Flora had had enough. They went on to talk about cars, golf, wives, anything but the surgery, his progress, and more importantly his discharge date.

It was too much as she still had to write up the case notes before she could go home. Flora butted in and enquired about him going home. Mr Atherton cleared his throat and proceeded to bite her head off. He stated that he couldn't possibly go home on a Friday; his wife would never let him rest. He'd had major surgery a few more days would be more acceptable. His Consultant agreed. Flora was fuming by now, she was tired and hungry, and time was ticking on. She had to get her boys to school. There was nothing wrong with him she mumbled to herself leaving the room. He could do everything that was expected for this stage of the surgery. This was typical of this hospital. Flash your cash you can do what you want.

Flora hadn't met this man before but knew she never wanted set eyes on him again. He had made her so angry and very late.

Yet here she was 3 years later finding this man fascinating. It didn't add up.

Flora had celebrated her birthday since her last night shift. She told him that a few friends, her mum and she had been to see "The Dream Toppings" male strippers for a giggle. He laughed and wanted to know all about her family, her interests, her hopes and dreams.

Flora hadn't realised how long they had been talking until one of the other patients rang their bell for assistance.

Flora's shift went really quickly. There was so much more she wanted to know about this man more so as John was being discharged home in the morning. Flora went into say goodbye at the end of her shift.

He asked her if he could take her out for dinner sometime in the future, just as a thank you he'd said, for all she had done for him over the past 10 days.

Flora informed him that it really wasn't necessary or the done thing. It was not ethical and they could both get into trouble if word got out.

"Well", he said "I'm not going to say anything are you"?

"No" she replied. "Don't suppose I am".

"Ok. Then let me call you and we will take it from there shall we" he said.

She gave him her home number and left his room.

Flora couldn't believe she had just agreed to that. He won't ring he was just being kind. Why would he want to? Why am I even thinking like this or about him? She thought to herself as she drove home and pulled up into her drive.

The days weeks and months rolled on. Flora went about her life as usual. Busily juggling her home and working life around her son's.

Although her shifts could be really busy and stressful at times she loved her job and couldn't ever imagine doing anything else. It was the most rewarding job in her mind. But after eighteen years of nursing, and, the majority of her shifts being spent on night duties, she thought may be it was time to try her hand at working the day shifts. Her son's less needy of her now had their own social lives. It could benefit them all one way or another. Flora had approached her ward manager several times over the past few months but as there were no vacancies, it wasn't looking too hopeful for the time being.

It was early December and Flora had taken a week's holiday. But as she had worked the beginning of the week and wasn't scheduled to go back until the weekend after her holiday, it worked out to more than two weeks before she had to return to work. It gave her plenty of time to prepare for Christmas catch up with old friends and be there for her boys.

She was busy preparing tea when the telephone rang.

It was her ward manager asking Flora if she would like to do a day shift the following day in practice for her new contract starting in the New Year.

Did she hear right? Had she got a day job at last?

It was to be a 3pm-11pm shift. Flora was having difficulty taking this all in. Such a surprise and so unexpected she asked if she could phone her back in 10mins when she could get her head around it all..

Wow, she thought, so exciting. She had composed herself and about to dial the hospital number when the phone rang again.

It was John.

"Hello. Flora is that you"? "Yes", she replied

"Hi this is John. I'm not disturbing you?"

"No not at all, what a lovely surprise, lovely to hear from you" she said. Two surprises in a space of ten minutes, aren't I the lucky one she thought

"How are you? How's work"? What have you been up to?" he asked.

"Well where do I start" she said. I am fine, work is fine, I'm on annual leave at the moment but have just been asked to work a late shift tomorrow. I was just about to phone back with the answer when you phoned.

"Well," he said, "I hope you're going to say yes because I am going back in tomorrow for an operation on my shoulder would be lovely to see you again".

"Yes I was actually. I am going to be moving to day shifts from 5th January anyway so my manager thought this would be good experience for me." She said.

"Great". He said. "See you tomorrow then. I will look forward to it."

"Me to" she said. "I'll go in a little earlier and come and find you before my shift.

Flora was totally over whelmed by it all. She returned the call to the hospital and replaced the receiver quite excited. As she continued in preparing the supper she was in quite a daze.

At two thirty Flora stepped out of the changing room and headed down onto the ward. She looked at the admission list and found Jon had been allocated to room 6. Tapping his door, "surprise" she said as she entered his room.

Flora. "Hello come in, how lovely to see you. You look amazing he said. He walked over to greet her and kissed her cheek.

"Hi. How are you? What time are you going to theatre? She asked.

"4pm, he said so not long now. Which ward are you working on this afternoon?"

I'm downstairs but I can pop up and see you I'm sure. She said.

They chatted until it was time for Flora's shift to start.

Flora left the room and headed downstairs to commence her shift. She felt happy, excited, nervous and apprehensive all at the same time.

The girls on the ward welcomed her to day duty and proceeded to hand over the patients she would be responsible for during the next 8 hours. She felt really nervous now. There were patients that needed admitting and then preparing for theatre. Patients were returning from theatre needing care and an eye kept on and patients who were ready to be discharged waiting for their paperwork. The routine followed on the day shift was completely different to what she had been used to on her night shift. Nights were so much more laid back so much quieter in respect of no visitors, telephones, ringing constantly or interruptions from well just about anyone it seemed.. How was she going to cope? Was she going to like it? There were visitors walking back and forth asking for room numbers, receptionist she had never met before asking her questions she didn't always know the answers to. Telephones appeared to be constantly ringing. It was so noisy

Mary, her best friend and sister-in-charge, put her arm around her. "Don't worry; she said you will be fine. We have all been here

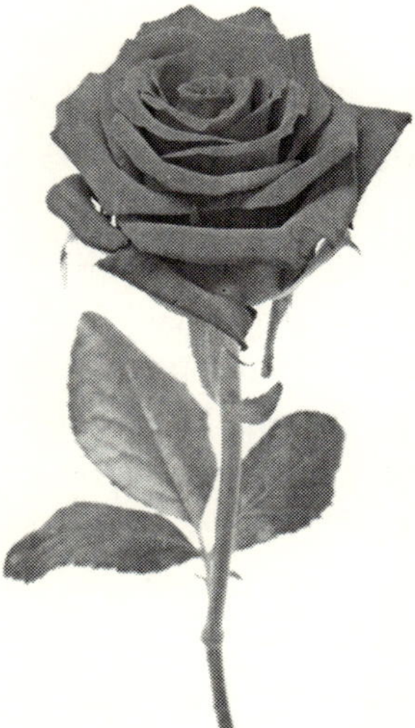

so understand how you're feeling. If you are not sure of anything come and find one of us" "Thanks" said Flora.

Once handover had finished Flora went about organising her work load. She introduced herself to her patients, looked at charts. Made notes. She had two patients going to theatre so went to make sure they were all ready to go. Chatted to the visitors. Day duty was a real eye opener. A different working life than what she had been used to. Flora had just returned to the ward after discharging one of her patients helping him into the back of his wife's car. Sister asked if she wanted to go with her colleague to theatre to take and collect a patient. "Good experience for when you have to take yours later that evening". She said

On her way back she managed to pop in and check on John. Although he had not long been back on the ward and was still very sleepy he appeared to be fine.

At 6pm Consultants, who had been operating that afternoon, and those on their way home for the day, made their final visits to their patients, giving any new instructions for care to the staff. Suppers were given out. The drug rounds commenced. The next two hours appeared to go really quickly. Flora was sent to supper. Meals were provided for the staff there was a choice of hot or cold meals, salads and jacket potatoes desserts to die for fruit and yoghurt. So much to choose from but only 15mins to eat it in therefore Flora opted for the salad and Jacket potato. It hadn't been a bad shift so far. I think I am going to enjoy days she thought to herself as went about eating her supper.

The ward started quietening down in preparation for the evening and the night shifts arrival. Flora's shift didn't finish until 11pm but

knowing the night routine so well, Flora began do the work for her colleagues. She laid up the linen trolleys. Prepared admission bed statements for the morning receptionists, turned back the bedding ready for the patients to get into bed. dimmed the room lights. All that was left for her colleagues to do now was the medicine rounds. She had even laid up a tray of coffee for them for when they came out of report.

There wasn't really any more she could do once the night staff had arrived.

With the night's sister's permission Flora went up to room 6 to spend some time with John until her shift ended.

He was awake now and pleased to see her and was looking forward to hearing all about her experience on the day shift. They chatted right up until the end of her shift. His surgery had gone well and he hadn't been given a morphine pump. The time had just flown by, she got up from her chair and began making tracks to go home and let John get the rest he needed.

John was a lot older than her. He had is own studio at the bottom of his garden where many shoots took place that he promised to show her one day. He was married, in not a particularly happy marriage, to his third wife. Leading separate lives under the same roof seemed a strange arrangement to Flora. But it seemed to work for them. His step daughter had given him two adorable grandchildren who lived abroad and he got to see them twice a year.

Flora was in her mid thirties and had two little boys. She had been married for sixteen years to a man she had first met at school. He was a lovely man who gave her everything she wanted, freedom to come and go as she wanted. She had a strong network of friends and family, but had a feeling there was something missing from her life. She couldn't explain it or even describe the feeling that she had of not really belonging or would be staying in her house for longer than was necessary. She had never really felt inspired or enthusiastic enough to want to decorate or put her mark on the house. It was as though she was on loan until the time was right for her move on to where ever that might be.

Flora had managed to visit John while he was still in hospital.

He had recovered well and was due to be discharged the next day just in time for Christmas.

He was unable to drive for 6weeks, but they had arranged to meet as soon as his physiotherapist, Consultant said his shoulder had healed and it was ok to do so.

Flora started her new position on January 5th. She found the shifts busy but was enjoying the challenge. She met staff who had worked in the hospital for almost the same amount of years that she had only they had never met. She was introduced to Consultants she hadn't seen for along while as the new girl who had been working there for 10 years already. Her world had been opened up to new experiences both at work and at home. Her boys had become used to letting themselves in from school and playing, watching T.V. until their dad arrived home. She did feel guilty at times for working during the day and leaving them but had noticed how grown up they were becoming, less dependent in some ways.

Later in the week John telephoned to say he had seen the Consultant who had said if all continues to go well he would be able to drive from next week. "That's great news" said Flora.

"I thought so" said John

"So if you have some free time next week how about meeting me for a coffee or lunch somewhere?"

"That would be lovely. I am free on Thursday" she replied

They arranged to meet in a local country pub not far from where Flora lived at 1230pm.

It was a lovely spring day. Flora, excited and anxious pulled up outside the pub and waited for John to arrive. She had forgotten to ask what sort of car he drove so she just had to sit and wait for him to arrive. Half an hour went by and there had been no sign of him. She had no telephone number or any means of contacting him she hadn't needed to as he had always phoned her. If she went and he arrived she would feel awful. If he had stood her up she would feel stupid for sitting there waiting. Her mind was doing over time, her stomach cartwheels. People were going in and out of the pub noticing she was still sitting there in the car park. What should she do?

In the next few minutes a 4x4 pulled up along side her. He was here and so apologetic for keeping her waiting.

He explained he had taken a wrong turning and had to drive miles out of his way to turn round due to the narrow lanes and the size of his vehicle.

You're here now and that was all that mattered she said, as she got out of her car. He looked so different in his day clothes not at all as she had imagined. She had only ever seen him in his dressing gown and pyjamas.

He commented how attractive she looked as they made their way inside the pub.

They found a nice quiet table at the far end of the room. John had informed her that he would be celebrating his birthday the day before their date and flora had remembered this. Once they had sat down and ordered their food she handed him a card. He was surprised she had remembered. Really pleased she had been so thoughtful. He reached over and squeezed her hand. Flora's tummy flipped over.

They had chatted for ages' exchanging long glances at each other.Because of John's late arrival flora was more conscious of the time. It was limited it enough but now it was quickly slipping by, she had to collect her boys from school. Their food arrived and as they finished their coffee Flora reached over and gave John her mobile number. "Probably easier to call me on this" she said to him.

As they walked backed to their cars John asked if he could see her again. Flora wanted to say no because it isn't right but found herself saying yes to him. He promised to call her to arrange something soon.

What was happening? Flora wasn't sure, but as she followed him back along the road she knew she couldn't wait for their next meeting.

At the junction just before her village, John stopped and got out of his jeep. He walked towards her car. Flora rolled down her window.

He popped his head inside and kissed her. Wow! She thought. Kissing him back she just melted.

"I'll call you later" he said. Returning to his car.

Flora's head was all over the place now. What had she done? She hadn't had that much attention or felt this alive for along while.

Composing herself, as the sound of a car horn rang in her ears from behind, she drove off in the direction of her house.

What's, that smell mum? Her boys asked as they stepped though the front door.

Flora had felt so guilty for feeling alive and enjoying herself so much

She had gone straight home and cleaned her house from top to bottom with bleach. A way of trying to justify even erase the past few hours.

"Oh I've been spring cleaning" she told them. "It smells awful" they replied.

At 5pm her mobile rang. It was John. She went upstairs so as not to be heard by the boys.

"Hello" she said.

"Hi. I just wanted to say thank you for your company. I had a lovely time. It was lovely to see you. When are you free again?" He said.

"Not until next Friday now" she said.

"Ok, then next Friday it will be then, oh assuming you had no other plans?" he said.

Even if she had she would be cancelling them for sure. She wanted to be with him.

"No I don't think so" she said

"Ok, so what would you like to do, where would like to go?"

What would be your ideal date? He said.

"All these decisions". She said back.

Well let me think, 007 dressed in a tuxedo, a private jet flying to the most romantic place on earth, champagne flowing, whilst lying back on satin sheets and fluffy cushions admiring the view. Both inside and out!

But as we haven't got that much time, I'll settle for you a can of coke and a park bench, "oh you decide, surprise me" she said.

He rang off. But that wasn't the last she heard from him. Their phone calls and text messages were becoming more frequent. Each morning as she turned on her phone, Flora had a message from him, wishing her a good shift/ day. At the end of each shift he would call her to see how she was how her day had been. They were fast becoming very much apart of each others lives and somehow it felt right to both of them.

John had obviously taken on board what Flora had said with regards to their date. He asked her to meet him in a small country village not far from where he lived. He gave her directions as it was unfamiliar territory to her. As she pulled up she smiled. There he was dressed in a black tux, white shirt, black bow tie, carrying a red rose. He walked towards the car, opened the door and helped her out. They said nothing as he presented her with the rose. Taking and kissing the back of her hand, he led her to the little hotel.

Unknown to Flora, John knew the owner so he had arranged everything prior to our date.

John led her into the bedroom. No detail had been left out, well apart from the sea view; there was champagne set in ice in a silver bucket. Soft music was playing and fragrant candles burning. Rose petals had been scattered on the bed. Flora was in heaven. She had to be as nothing had ever happened to her like this before.

"You did all this for me? I don't know what say".

As she continued to take it all in, her favourite song played on the radio, Perfect Moment. Tears filled her eyes. I shall remember this for ever. This is my perfect moment" she said. Thank you so much, reaching up to kiss him. There were hundreds of tea-lights lit all around the room. He had thought of everything.

She turned to look at him. He took her in his arms and they walked towards the bed. They knew what they were doing was wrong but it felt so right.

He caressed her so tenderly, kissing the back of her neck, her cheeks her eye lids. As he kissed the top of her head and held her in his arms, Flora wanted to explode. Looking longingly into his eyes he undressed her and laid her on the bed. Joining her they knew they had connected on a very high level, this was the beginning of something very special between them.

It was beautiful. He was beautiful and Flora felt safe in his arms. Nothing mattered anymore. As long as they had each other they would cope with anything life had to throw at them.

There was a knock on the door. John got up. That will be lunch he explained. I hope you like salmon? He really had thought of everything. Today had changed their lives more than they had both realised. They began spending more and more time together. They visited places of interest, drove to the seaside, walked in the country or just took time out to

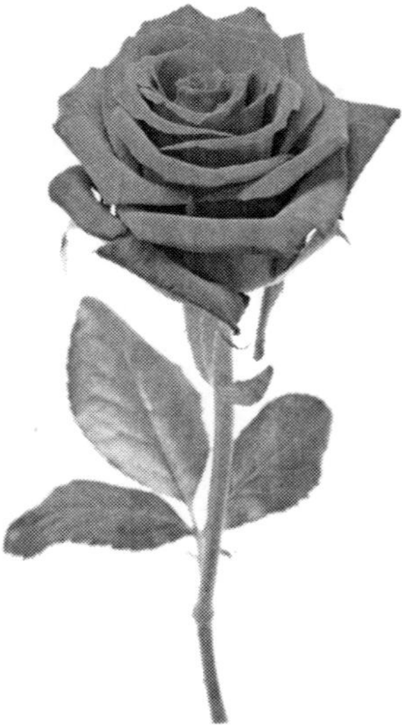

relax in the car when there were only minutes they could snatch to be together.

The anniversary of their first date was approaching. John was going to be away on a photo shoot. Flora often thought back to the very first time she set eyes on John and how for no apparent reason has taken an instant dislike to him. She still didn't understand it. Found it even more difficult explaining it to John who thought it funny.

"How would you like to come with me" he said "Come with you? She said. How can I come with you"? "It's impossible, but thank you for thinking of me. It was a nice thought" she said.

"Well I'm a great believer in fate. He said. If it is meant to be something will happen that will allow you to come.

"If only" she said

."Someone is looking after us" she said as John answered his phone. I have been invited to a hospital reunion on that Saturday. "Hi honey slow down, he said. start again"

An invitation arrived today!. Apparently it is 20 years since I qualified. There is to be a reunion with accommodation provided that same weekend you wanted me to go to the photo shoot with you" she said again. "There you go. He said. Its fate what did I tell you. It's meant to be."

The fashion shoot was in a hotel overlooking the sea on the south coast. She had seen the brochure. It was beautiful and very expensive if the tariffs were anything to go by. She was going to be thoroughly spoilt. Flora was very excited but she couldn't help wandering how she would be able to pull this off. She had sent her apologies to the organiser of the reunion but was still acting as if she was going to her family. Although she felt awful and knew she was doing wrong, she felt amazingly calm about it all. Surprisingly every thing leading up to that weekend fell in to place almost without her trying. This is all too good to be true. She thought. She was just an ordinary wife and mother after all. Flora felt it was time she confided in someone, Just in case something happened while she was away.

Her friend was also a nurse. They had trained together and known each other for years but Flora wasn't sure how the news would go down. She felt she needed Jayne, who was going to the reunion, to know why she wouldn't be going and would be able to fill her in on the events of that night as well as being a contact, cover.

Although shocked at Flora's secret, Jayne understood and was happy to cover for her. She knew if roles were reversed Flora would do the same for her. Her next dilemma, what was she going to wear?

The weekend had arrived the weather was perfect. Flora drove to John's friend's house where they had arranged to leave her car. She had been introduced to him in hospital on occasions he had been in to visit John. When John arrived they made their way to the hotel.

"Happy" he said squeezing her hand. "Very" she said as they drove off.

At the hotel they were shown to their room. Flora now felt as though she was playing out somebody else's life. This didn't feel real a 5 stars plus hotel. Nothing was too much trouble for the waiters.

John had to go and check the itinerary for the shoot. "Order whatever you like" he said to Flora. "We have a tab; it is all charged to the company just phone room service I won't be long".

Flora put down her bag and started to explore the room. It was a large room with a king sized bed. There was a TV, coffee making, facilities a beautiful view of the sea from the large window to the side of the room. She could see people walking along the cliffs enjoying the sunshine. Surfers riding the waves. In the bathroom there was a walk-in shower, a corner bath with soft fluffy white towels. "Freebies" as she called them, small bottles of shampoo and bubble-bath donned the shelf above the sink. She could get used to this.

As she unpacked her bag John came back into the room.

"This is heaven she said as she threw herself on to the bed. "Look at that view it's beautiful. Can we go for a walk she asked?"

"Not right now honey. Maybe we will have time later. I have to go to work. Come with me". He said. I'll introduce you to the crew.

The team of floor managers, light engineers, make-up artists, wardrobe and John's right hand man who changed the camera lenses in between shots, made her feel very welcome. Each explained their part in the process. The models, some as young as her boys, were stunning and very professional. The shoot was for summer clothes, soon to be available in a well known catalogue.

Flora was fascinated. John had spoken often about these people and now here she was watching them all at work.

John caught her eye, smiled and winked. She felt reassured and proud to be there. He was very passionate about his work that's for sure.

The time flew by. Flora had enjoyed every moment. The manager called time for that day and 8am start was agreed for the morning.

With cameras packed away and equipment tidily left John and Flora made their way up to their room to change. The team were free to do as they wished this evening. Some were just happy to chill in the bar. A few lived locally and went home. Flora and John decided to have a walk along the beach before dinner. The stars were shinning, the air was still. The sound of the waves lapping onto the beach was so calming and peaceful. As he took her hand she felt she was in heaven. This was a moment Flora had always dreamt about with the hero she had always dreamt of being with. Now here she was living the dream with her hero for real.

"Wow! "You look stunning. I can't believe my eyes you gorgeous creature" he said to Flora as he came out of the bathroom.

Flora had changed into a backless black clingy dress wearing high heels. Something she didn't wear that often but as John was over 6 foot tall her neck ached on occasions reaching up to kiss him.

"I am one lucky guy. If things were different I marry you tomorrow before someone else snapped you up". He said

John walked over to his bag and pulled out a box.

"Happy anniversary" he said.

"Thank you. You shouldn't have" she said opening the box. Inside was a beautiful white gold necklace inserted with tiny blue stones.

Blue Topaz to match your eyes" he said. As he fastened the necklace around her neck" kissing it as if to seal the deal.

As he led her to the dinning room she felt like a princess. They danced the night away oblivious to the world around them. It was a fairy tale come true for Flora she had had a ball but like all good things the weekend was over all too soon. The shoot had gone well. Flora and John went home back to their normal life and routines.

Sitting outside the church the memories of that weekend and other special moments they had spent together became too much for her. The stars were shinning, the air was still, I still remember, I always will. And now I've lost the hero that I dreamed of. Tears filled her eyes as she remembers more of the reading.

"You know he was scared" the clairvoyant said. Scared to do the right thing and commit to you. He is saying he should have tried harder.

Feared what he stood to loose rather than stood to gain being with you.

He had nothing to offer you other than his unconditional love. He said you deserved more. He is quite emotional he is bringing tears to my eyes. She said. I love you so much and that hasn't diminished since I physically left you, in fact it is even stronger, if that is possible. I wanted to give you so much, but I've failed to leave you even the smallest inheritance. And I know you will understand why it had to be like that. What I am able to give you is the love vibration from spirit. This is worth far more than anything in the material world. My darling I loved to buy you flowers and now I send you beautiful white roses and lilies for pure love. Our love. Don't waste your time pursuing shadows what will be will be without any further effort from you. I will always be with you, on holidays, at work, remembering all our good times together in the sun. But it was all too short, too short.

I will find you someone who will treat you and love you as you deserve. You will have to let me go though otherwise it won't stand a chance. Dance my lovely and enjoy yourself. I do hear your thoughts darling. Talk to me more. We used to talk loads on the phone when I was alive. We can talk for free now". We did spend hours talking thought Flora smiling to herself.

"I will your ears will ache so much you'll see" she said out loud. He is fading now the medium told her. He is showering you in red roses. "Thank you" said Flora. "He was very serious wasn't he" she said. "He wanted you to know how it was for him. And this was his time to tell you. The medium replied".

John and Flora had certainly made the most of their precious time together. Quality not Quantity had been the key to their relationship. They complimented each other so well. Little did they know it would come to an end in quite the way it did.

More cars arrived outside the church. Flora looked at her watch. Her friends would be here soon.

The summer came and went. John had gone to Spain for Christmas but had returned ill. "It's probably due to climate change his doctor had said. You'll be ok in a day or to I'm sure"

But he wasn't. By February John had been ill for several weeks and was now experiencing chest pains, coughing and generally feeling unwell. Flora had advised him to go back and see his G.P. His appointment had been that morning. John was on his way to hospital when he telephoned her to say that an E.C.G, tracing of his heart, appeared abnormal and his GP would like a second opinion from a cardiologist. He told her would phone as soon as he had news.

Fortunately it was normal but he had been put on antibiotics for a possible chest infection and had been advised to stay in hospital for further investigations.

This worried Flora. Being in the nursing profession wasn't always in her best interest when it came to people she cared about. "What if's" started playing on her mind.

At moments like this the reality of what they were doing hit home. But there was nothing they could do. He had a wife and she had to be with him, Even though they didn't always see eye to eye.

A few days later John phoned. Flora was at work so couldn't take the call. John had left a message saying he would meet her

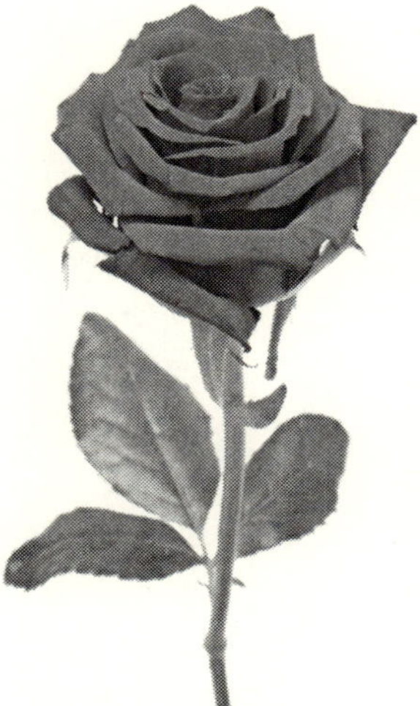

at the usual place at 2pm unless he heard differently. Her text back confirmed she would be there.

Excited she made her way into the café but when she saw him she was horrified. He looked so poorly. His face was grey. Flora couldn't believe her eyes. He had lost weight over the past two weeks too.

"They are not happy with me" he said as he kissed her, I need more tests, my chest isn't good and the antibiotics haven't had any effect"

That's got to be good then, at least we can get to the root of the problem get you back to your old self". Said Flora, "I hope so" he said ordering the coffee.

John had been referred to a physcian specialising in heart and lungs. He was to have a Broncoscopy (camera fed down into the lungs) the following Monday in order to find out what was going on. Why this cough was not resolving. Flora checked her diary. She was working that day but promised to call in on him on her way home as he was going to be in the private ward of the NHS hospital.

She knew his wife wouldn't be visiting until later in the evening.

Half an hour before her shift came to an end Flora text John. She had tried phoning his room earlier but he had not answered. How r u? Will be over shortly Xx

Nothing could have prepared Flora for the reply that came back.

Hello darling. Looking forward to seeing you, not good news! I have 8 weeks to live. X x

"8 weeks no it can't be right". It can't be. She burst into tears.

"Whatever is the matter? Said Mary who happened to be passing by

"He has 8weeks". Flora told her.

"Who has"? Said Mary

"John. Mary I need to tell you something but right now I need to go. I'll call you later".

"Are you alright?" Said Mary

"No. she said I'm not". I'll explain later"

Flora headed straight to his room she found John sitting on his bed staring in to space. "I'm so sorry darling I'm so sorry I am going to leave you". How she kept her composure she didn't know, her heart had just been broken into tiny little pieces. Her world turned upside down.

She fell into his arms and they cried, not saying a word they just held each other. Breaking away he told her that the broncoscopy had shown he had cancer in both lungs. The coughing and chest pain he had been suffering was an indication of how rapidly the cancer was advancing and why the antibiotics hadn't helped him.

"I have such a lot to do before I go. I have already started to plan the funeral. I have phoned the undertakers I want to price it all. I'll have to leave her the money. She is no good with money". John was now pacing around the room talking to himself.

This was all going to fast for Flora. Hello. What about me she thought I'm in this to. She couldn't think straight. She still is trying to take it all in.

"Does she know Flora asked him"?

"Yes but she isn't coming in I wanted this time with you, get used to the idea". I can't face her right now". He said.

This won't be easy on you darling I know and I'm sorry but have so much to sort out. I may not be able to see you or phone you so often. She will see to that she will be fussing watching over me even more"

"I know, I understand". She said trying to be brave. Inside she was hurting. She was about to loose her best friend and the best thing that had ever happened to her.

"I will get Nick to keep you posted and to act a go between for us". It's the best I can do.

They had agreed that Flora would drive him home on his day of discharge. As it would probably be the last time she would see him they were planning to have lunch on route. She picked him up as planned on the Thursday morning. Not a word was said as they drove towards his home and the pub.

She fought hard to keep the tears in her eyes from falling.

He tried to make her laugh about this being "the last supper". "Don't joke please, she said. This is so hard for me. How am I going to cope with out you?" Neither of them knew what to say to each other. They eat their lunch in silence almost like strangers meeting for the first time. It was awkward as they both knew that this would be the first time they would have to say goodbye forever.

Walking away was the hardest thing she had ever done.

No phone calls no planned visits to look forward to. Nothing but emptiness filled her soul now. She felt lost didn't quite know what to say or do. He held her, she held on so tight never wanting to ever let go. She wanted to scream don't leave me, tell me it isn't true! But what good would it have done. Trying not to cry she broke away and said goodbye. She got into her car and drove off as quickly as she could without looking back. She didn't want his last memory of her to be one of her sobbing.

Flora's heart was breaking; the pain was unbearable she thought she was going to die. There was no –one she could turn to no one to hold her now and make it feel better. She was alone in every sense of the word.

Home was an hour away. This was all the time she had to compose herself and go about things as though nothing had happened.

Somehow she had to start putting her life back together. How she was going to do it she didn't know.

Mary had been so understanding and had wished she could have been there for her the day she said goodbye to John. She became Flora's rock when the going got tough. She told Flora she would make sure she was there to support her on the day of John's funeral also along with her only other friend who knew what had been going on.

Three weeks after saying goodbye to John, Nick phoned her to say that he was bringing John into town to deal with a few legal issues. "John was hoping he could see you? He said. He's missing you".

"Say yes" she said. She knew this would be opening wounds again but she had to see him for his sake and hers.

Nick bought John to the little coffee shop where they used to meet.

He looked tired and so thin. It was all he could do to talk as his breathing had become difficult. He was pleased to see her. They chatted for a little while until he felt the need to go home and rest.

"Keep smiling. He said it's that smile that keeps me going"

I will. She said back to him.

He had deteriorated quickly since the day she took him home. Flora hoped his passing would be sooner rather than later. She didn't want him to suffer any more than he had to. She would have given anything to have been able to nurse him until the end and at whatever the cost to her and her family.

Flora had planned trips, days out with friends and family as part of her "moving on and coping" plan. This gave her something to focus on in the time leading up to the day the "phone call from Nick" came and beyond.

The first of those trips was to see a concert that coming weekend.. Her friends had organised a night away. Going Friday morning and coming back on the Saturday afternoon. She was looking forward to it. John had bought her the CD of this group for Christmas.

They had a fantastic time shopping, seeing the sights, the concert and plenty of good food and wine. She had noticed several missed calls on her phone. Anonymous caller was all it said no message left.

She called home to see if everything was ok there. It was. "Don't worry they'll call back or would have left you a message if it was that urgent" her friends said. "Yeah s'pose your right" said Flora.

Not long after Flora arrived home she received a text message. It was from John.

He had been admitted back in to hospital. He was going into his 8th week now. Oh my god. She thought.

What should she do? In her heart she knew she wanted to be with him but the reality would mean having to tell her husband what had been going on. Did she want to see him at this late stage of his illness, yes she did she had wanted to nurse him until the end. Maybe this is fate again working her magic.

She decided to go and deal with the consequences later. It was no more than he would do for her if the tables had been reversed.

She text him back telling him she was on her way.

He had been admitted because he was in so much pain and had been unable to pass urine for 12 hours. It was obvious to Flora that his organs were now failing. He had been catheterised but very little urine had been drained. He wanted her reassurance. Her hand to hold and give him the strength he needed right now. As he rested Flora told him about her weekend and the concert she had been to. She discovered it had been his missed calls. He was phoning from the hospital just after he had been admitted.

Flora stayed for an hour before she made her way back home. She promised to return tomorrow. John had made it known to everyone that he wanted to die at home and would only stay in hospital until his pain was under control. His wife didn't like hospitals or driving at night so only visited in the mornings. This made flora angry. Why she couldn't have made an exception at this late stage of her husbands illness she didn't know. She didn't like to think of him being alone when she couldn't be there.

Flora was on a late shift the next day. When she arrived at work she found there were only 7 patients to care for and 4 staff. She didn't want to be there doing nothing when she could be spending precious time with John. Flora had 6hours time owing so she asked if she could take back that time right now. "If anyone phones for me at work, she said, say I'm busy then phone me on my mobile". Fortunately she didn't have to explain why.

And at 3 O'clock Flora left to be at John's bedside where she stayed until the end of her shift. There wasn't a lot more they could say to each other. Being together was all that mattered to them now as they both knew his time was slipping away. He held her hand as he drifted in and out of sleep reassured knowing she was there. As she watched him breathing she remembered all their good times together.

Flora didn't know how little time John had left but as she got up to leave she promised him she would return tomorrow before he went home. Knowing full well, it would be for the last time.

In the early hours of the next morning Flora's mobile rang. It was the hospital. He is asking for you the staff nurse informed her please come as quickly as you can. We have phoned for his wife. She said.

Flora, trying not to panic, got up and made her way to the hospital. She didn't live to far away certainly a lot nearer than his wife who would have had to get someone to bring her in as she didn't night drive.

She entered his room. He had deteriorated and didn't have long. She took his hand and whispered I'm here. It's ok now. He managed to squeeze her hand. She kissed him and held him in her arms.

Flora, being the kind caring nurse that she was, had hoped his wife would make it on time. But it was not meant to be. John slipped away in her arms fifteen minutes later. When he had been first diagnosed Flora would have given anything to have nursed him, been with him when he died but knew that would never have been possible. But someone had been watching over them that night for sure because they were together and her wish had come true.

"Tap, tap came on the window. Flora came back into the here and now.

Hello Flora we have arrived. U ok? Her friends' Mary and Jane asked.

Flora got out of her car.

"Yes as ok as I can be" she said

They made there way into the church. The coffin was already in there draped in the union flag. Flora had bought a small bunch of flowers with her. She placed them on top of the coffin.

"You can't do that Flora" her friends said. Family flowers only!

"Well I can't take them back now". She said. Her bouquet of flowers had been placed beside the coffin but she couldn't stop and look at them without drawing attention to herself.

They made their way to the back of the church and sat down.

Flora remembers everything John had said about the funeral. People he had described were behaving just as he'd said they would.

As the end of the very long catholic service came to an end, the sign that John had told her to look out for happened.

The flowers and drapes were removed from the coffin; the mourners took their position either side and began carrying him out of the church towards the waiting Hurst. As they made their way towards the door Flora noticed the flowers. Hers were the only ones lying on the top of the coffin and there it was amongst the flowers she'd sent to the undertakers, the single pink rose.

The burial was for his family only. Nick had managed to give her directions to the burial ground a few miles away before the service. All she needed to do now was to go there and retrieve the rose. She had planned to do this the next day when things had quietened down and she could be alone with her own thoughts. She found there were many poses and bouquets of flowers covering the spot where he was buried. A beautiful view of the hills and fields made it feel so tranquil and peaceful up there. The sun was shinning, this was in a good place she thought. Flora retrieved the rose.

Fly, Fly little wing,
Rest in peace my sweet darling,
Fly away for the time is right,
Go now honey, find the light.
I will not cry as I now have prove
That some loves last forever.

You were my hero John the one I dreamed of.

Flora knew this wasn't goodbye.
They would find their own way of communicating and continue to be together forever.

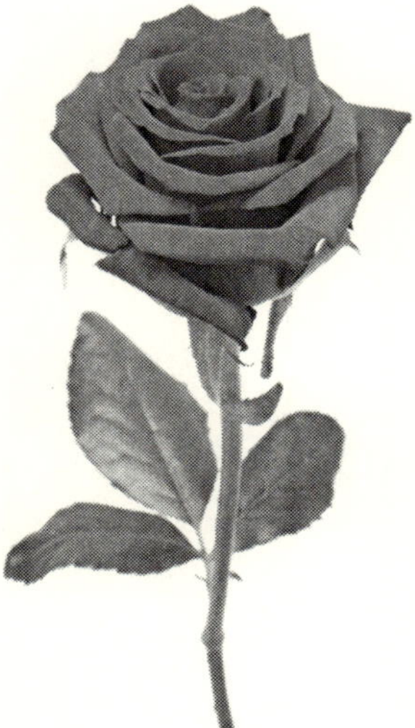

Printed in the United States
220700BV00001B/26/P